Greta Gorsuch

THE NIGHT
TELEPHONE

Greta Gorsuch has taught ESL/EFL and applied linguistics for more than thirty years in Japan, Vietnam, and the United States. Greta's work has appeared in journals such as *System*, *Reading in a Foreign Language*, *Language Teaching*, *Language Teaching Research*, and *TESL-EJ*. Her books in the Gemma Open Door Series include *The Cell Phone Lot*, *Key City on the River*, *Post Office on the Tokaido*, and *Queen Serene*. Greta lives in beautiful wide West Texas and goes camping whenever she can.

First published by Gemma in 2021.

Gemma
230 Commercial Street
Boston MA 02109 USA

www.gemmamedia.org

©2021 by Greta Gorsuch

Printed in the United States of America

978-1-936846-93-1

Library of Congress Cataloging-in-Publication Data

Names: Gorsuch, Greta, author.
Title: The night telephone / Greta Gorsuch.
Description: Boston, MA : Gemma, 2021. | Series: Gemma open door
Identifiers: LCCN 2021018069 (print) | LCCN 2021018070 (ebook) | ISBN
   9781936846931 (trade paperback) | ISBN 9781936846948 (ebook)
Classification: LCC PS3607.O77 N55 2021 (print) | LCC PS3607.O77 (ebook)
   | DDC 813/.6--dc23
LC record available at https://lccn.loc.gov/2021018069
LC ebook record available at https://lccn.loc.gov/2021018070

Cover by Laura Shaw Design

Gemma's Open Doors provide fresh stories, new ideas, and essential resources for young people and adults as they embrace the power of reading and the written word.

GEMMA

Open Door

Thanks to Mr. Harsh S.

CHAPTER ONE

It was 2:00 a.m. Dr. Tarak Kapoor was wide awake. He had arrived at the Garnet, Texas, airport five days ago. He should be on Texas time by now. He should be sleeping better. But he wasn't. He was still on India time. His brain thought it was lunchtime in Mumbai. His body thought it was the middle of the day. He thought of his favorite place to eat lunch in Mumbai, in his old life. It was a small park outside the big, busy hospital where he worked. He would buy a bowl of rice and curry from a food truck outside the park. The cook would say hello. Then he would ask, in Hindi, "How many people stayed with us today?" Tarak would smile and

GRETA GORSUCH

say some number. It might be five. It might be twelve. There was always some number.

Tarak was a doctor at the Mumbai Royal Hospital. He took care of very sick people. He saved a lot of them. But some of them died, no matter what Tarak did. The food truck cook knew this. So when the cook asked, "How many people stayed with us today?" he really was asking how many people were alive under Tarak's care. The cook was trying to be positive. Tarak would then pay the man for his curry. He would find a shady spot and sit down to eat. The busy road outside the park seemed to disappear. Tarak could not hear the trucks and cars and motorbikes. He didn't hear their *beep! beep! beep!* horns.

2

He only heard the leaves on the trees moving. He ate slowly and enjoyed the spicy, rich curry.

Now, Tarak was thousands of miles away. In his dark room, Tarak turned over and closed his eyes. Then he opened them again. He turned on his other side. He kicked his blankets off. He tried to fall asleep. After another ten minutes he gave up. His neck hurt. His shoulders hurt. He got out of bed. All of that thinking about the curry was making him hungry. At 2:00 a.m.? Really? Hungry?

He walked through his apartment. There was a bedroom and a large living room/kitchen sort of thing. In the kitchen, he felt his way to the refrigerator. He opened it. The bright light

3

inside came on. Tarak blinked and rubbed his eyes. All he could see in the refrigerator was a banana and some milk. It would have to do. He took out the banana. He found a plastic cup and poured himself some milk. He sat down on the new carpet of his apartment and ate his snack.

His apartment was not very dark, he thought. His big front window now seemed almost bright. All around his apartment complex there were outdoor lights that made an orange glow. It looked so different from Mumbai. Mumbai was bright at night, too. But every building had different lights. Some were very bright and white. Others were dull and yellow.

Tarak's apartment complex in

Garnet was new and large. There was a fence all around it. The six parking lots were full of cars. Tarak didn't have a car. He would have to do something about that soon. He needed to drive so he could buy food. It turned out his apartment complex was two miles from a food store. He couldn't even get to his bank unless he wanted to walk quite far.

Tarak sighed. He had so much to do. He had so many new things to get used to. He had never guessed America would be like this. He really wanted to sleep. But it was clear he would not. He could lay in bed all night, and he would still be in India, where it was lunchtime.

Tarak decided to go out for a walk. Why not? He knew there was a major street not far away. He thought he knew how to get there and back. He put on his clothes and shoes. He put his key in his pocket. Then he walked out of his apartment. He found his way to the big front gate. The heavy thing swung shut behind him. Now he was on the street. After a few minutes' walk, he was in the cool darkness of Garnet on a summer night.

CHAPTER TWO

Tarak had an idea where to go. He went along a narrow street with houses and a few parked cars. There were trees, bigger than the ones at Tarak's apartment complex. The neighborhood seemed older. Some of the houses were very small. They were single family homes, not apartments. To Tarak's surprise, he could see lights on in a few of the houses. Other people were awake, too. Tarak wondered why. It was 2:30 a.m. He was not the only one who could not sleep.

Some dogs barked as Tarak passed. In the distance, he could hear sirens from a fire truck, or a police car. Even farther in the distance he heard a low sound, like a very large engine. Then he heard a long, long blast from a horn. Tarak smiled. He had it. It was a train. Tarak was hearing a train, far away somewhere in Garnet. It was just like India, only the American train horn sounded lower and longer. He kept walking in the cool darkness. Just a few blocks ahead he saw Thirty-Fourth Street. At least he thought it was Thirty-Fourth Street.

When his new colleague, Dr. Rick Becker, met him at the airport, Tarak could hardly keep his eyes open. Two days on a plane and five airports did that to you. Mumbai to Paris, to New York, to Houston, to Garnet. Rick drove through the bright sunlit streets. He said, "This is Thirty-Fourth Street. Your new apartment is pretty close by.

We'll be there in a few minutes." At the time, Tarak only said, "Yes, I see."

For the next several nights, Rick would pick Tarak up at his apartment. He would say where they were, naming the streets. One night they had dinner at a small Mexican restaurant. That was on University Avenue. Another night he drove Tarak by the big teaching hospital in town. That was on Fourth Street. Most often, though, they were on Thirty-Fourth Street. It was a major street. It was near Tarak's apartment.

As the days went by, Tarak began to wake up a little. He saw more and more. He saw that Thirty-Fourth Street had buildings of every shape and color. All the buildings were low. They were never more than one story high. But one was painted gray with a big yellow stripe. It was a coffee shop. Another was red brick with a bright blue door. It was a computer repair shop. Yet another, a flower shop, was painted pink.

Some Thirty-Fourth Street buildings had big windows and others had no windows. One building looked like a gas station. It had a large roof hanging over an open area big enough to drive a car into. Now it was a dry cleaner and laundry service. A lot of buildings on Thirty-Fourth Street looked empty, but then just as many had a small business in it. Tarak could hardly believe the variety of them. It reminded him of Mumbai. Somehow, he thought America would only have Walmarts and big box stores.

Tonight, Tarak left the darkness of the side street and came out on Thirty-Fourth Street. There were more streetlights here. They gave off a yellow glow. Off to the right, Tarak could see two sets of traffic lights. To the left, he saw five more sets of traffic lights, stretching far away. The closest one changed from red to green to yellow, and back to red. He watched that for a few minutes. There was not a single car or truck out. It was completely quiet. Tarak could hear the hum of the streetlights.

Suddenly, the traffic light he had been watching went dark. It was like someone just cut off the power. It was a little strange, Tarak thought. He would walk over. He didn't have anything else to do. When he got to the darkened traffic light he stood there for a few minutes. Across the street he saw the dry cleaner and laundry service, the one that had been an old gas station. It was closed. There was a faint light inside. He saw many rows of clean shirts and pants and dresses, waiting for their owners to come back for them. Then he noticed something else. To the right of the dry cleaner and laundry service was a telephone booth. The light was on, a bright white. Inside the booth was a black pay telephone.

CHAPTER THREE

Tarak laughed. A pay telephone? He couldn't believe it. Were there such things anymore? In the age of cell phones? This he had to see. He never thought he would see a pay telephone again. Especially in America. He looked each way so he could cross Thirty-Fourth Street. On his right, he saw a car coming. Something made him step back. Just behind him was a sewing shop, next to a comic book shop. Between the front doors of the two shops was something that looked like a park bench. Just a place for someone to sit. Overhead was a small roof. Tarak thought it would be nice for shade during Garnet's hot and bright days.

The car was coming closer. It was slowing down. Its turn signal went on. Tarak sat down on the bench behind him. He was in a little patch of darkness. The large, old dark car pulled over and parked in front of the dry cleaner and laundry service. The driver got out.

It was a woman, of medium height. She had dark hair, pulled back. Tarak could not see much more, except that the lady was wearing sunglasses. Who wore sunglasses at night? Was she afraid someone would recognize her? There was no one out. Except for Tarak in the darkness across the street, there was no one to see her. Was she crying? Was that why she was wearing sunglasses? Tarak couldn't hear her crying. And he wasn't about to let her know he was watching her. Any woman out at 3:00 a.m. would feel scared if a strange man tried to talk to her.

Somehow, Tarak was not surprised to see the woman walk over to the brightly lit phone booth. She opened the booth and then shut the door behind her. Through the glass, he saw her pick up the black telephone receiver. She put in some coins and dialed a number. Then she started to talk to someone. He couldn't hear any words. Just the lady's voice. It sounded like an ordinary conversation. She seemed to listen to someone on the other end. Then she would say something. Once she laughed. So the pay telephone worked. Tarak thought it might be a funny antique, just for show. Something like a piece of street art, that didn't really work.

The lady finished her call. She left the phone booth. She walked out to her car and got in. Through the driver's window, Tarak could see her take off her sunglasses. The lady wiped her eyes. She had been crying. Somehow, though, she looked happy, not sad. Who had she been talking to? What had they been talking about? She started her car and then drove away in the darkness.

Tarak was about to get up and walk across the street to see this strange pay telephone. Then he saw another car coming. This one came from the left. It was a small car, very quiet. As the car came closer, it slowed down. Its turn signal came on. Right in front of where

Tarak was sitting, the car pulled over and stopped. The engine went off. A young man got out. He saw Tarak and said, "Hey man." He didn't seem at all surprised to see Tarak. Tarak waved hello. The young man, who was tall and thin, walked across the street. He went to the phone booth. It still shone with a bright light. The man went inside the phone booth and picked up the black telephone receiver. He put in some coins. Then he started talking. Tarak heard him laugh.

The phone call was still going on twenty minutes later when Tarak checked his watch. He felt a wave of sleepiness. It was 3:30 a.m. He probably ought to get home. He started work the next morning at the telemedicine office.

It was going to be a big day. He got up and turned to walk down the dark street to his apartment complex. As far as he knew, the young man was still talking on the pay telephone on Thirty-Fourth Street, next to a set of traffic lights that didn't work.

CHAPTER FOUR

Tarak had a long and confusing day. It was his first day at Doctor's Choice Telemedicine. The whole day was training. Tomorrow there would be more lectures and workshops. Everyone wore masks due to the virus. At the end of the second day they would have practice sessions. Half of the new telemedicine doctors would be "patients." The other half would use Doctor's Choice Telemedicine technology to "see" the "patient" and give medical care. On the third day they would have a big test. They would "see" a *real* patient. They would be graded on their ability to give good medical care. Tarak thought that they would really be graded on how well they could communicate over a computer. Doctor's Choice Telemedicine already believed their new workers were good doctors.

Tarak had twenty-three new colleagues. All of them were young, like him. Many had just finished their medical training at hospitals. Everyone was from outside Garnet. They were young men and women of every shape, size, and color. At least five of Tarak's new colleagues were from another country. There were Jen and Antoine from Argentina, Adolfo from Brazil, and Emily from Taiwan. For Tarak, Jen, Antoine, Adolfo, and Emily, Doctor's Choice Telemedicine was their first job in the US.

Of course, any of the twenty-four

new telemedicine doctors could work anywhere if they had internet. But Doctor's Choice Telemedicine asked for all their new doctors to come for training in Garnet, Texas. It was the head office. Doctor's Choice Telemedicine made it easy for their doctors to live in Garnet, if they wanted to. They helped the new doctors find good apartments. For the first year, they paid housing costs and $5,000 toward buying a car.

Rick was there this morning. He was a tall African-American man, and also a new telemedicine doctor. His wife had gotten a job at the big university in Garnet. She and Rick had moved to Garnet eight months before. When Rick heard that Tarak was coming from overseas a week early and didn't have a car, he asked to meet Tarak at the airport. The office workers at Doctor's Choice Telemedicine were happy to give him Tarak's arrival time and flight number.

Jen, Antoine, Adolfo, Emily, and all of the other new telemedicine doctors had arrived only the day before. They were all staying at hotels. They blinked and yawned in the bright Garnet sunlight during their lunch break. They wanted to get outside so they could take off their masks.

They all walked together to a hamburger shop down the street. It was newly reopened after the shutdown from the virus. Everyone used the take-out window. Of course, Tarak could not eat hamburgers. One didn't eat beef in India. It just wasn't done. Rick said to the young girl at the takeout window, "Can you get my friend one of your fish sandwiches?" And in about five minutes, Tarak bit into the most delicious sandwich he had ever had. It had fresh, hot flaky fried fish, and a kind of sauce.

The hamburger shop had a place to eat outside. The new telemedicine doctors ate and talked. One of the American women, Lori, asked Tarak how he liked America. He said, "It's very fine so far. But I still cannot sleep. So I go out and walk at night, sometimes."

Lori asked, "What do you see? Aren't you afraid to be out by yourself?"

Tarak laughed and said, "Afraid? Not really. It's so quiet. No one is out. Although I think I have found out a mystery."

Now Rick was listening. "What kind of mystery?" he asked.

Tarak said, "When is the last time any of you saw a working pay telephone?"

CHAPTER FIVE

Tarak's question left his colleagues silent for a minute.

Antoine said, "There are still pay phones in Argentina. Not too many, though. Just in the really small towns."

"Uh-huh," Lori said. "We had them around when I was a kid. I haven't seen one in years. I'm not sure I would know how to use it!" Everyone at the table laughed.

One male colleague, Mark, told Tarak, Rick, and Lori how he had seen a video online. On the video, a man showed his two teenaged sons an old rotary-style telephone. The man in the video asked the boys to dial the phone number written on a piece of paper,

744-3137. Then the man left them to it. After ten minutes, the boys gave up. They had never done anything but push numbers on a cell phone screen. You could see their father in the background, laughing. The father, of course, had grown up with the old rotary dial telephones.

Rick wanted to know more. "What makes you ask? Are you saying you found an old pay telephone that works? In Garnet?"

Lori and Mark laughed hard. Lori was from Chicago, and Mark was from Boston. They had both been saying how small Garnet was. Lori had said, "Garnet's not the end of the earth, but you can see it from there!" Tarak had laughed and laughed at that. But he had seen something fascinating the night before. He thought there was more to Garnet than Lori thought.

Tarak answered, "Yes, I believe I have found such a telephone. And I think . . . it's the old-style phone Mark was talking about just now. You have to dial a number. Not push buttons. It's on Thirty-Fourth Street. Just a short walk from my apartment."

Rick said, "I'd like to see that."

Tarak said, "I'll show you after we're done today. I think I can find it."

"All right, then," Rick said.

For the rest of the day, the twenty-four new doctors took turns being "patients" and doctors. Tarak thought that the Doctor's Choice Telemedicine technology was easy to use. He could view a patient's list of medicines. He could see and talk to the patient. The video quality was not good. It would be hard to look closely at his patient's skin or eyes. What if they had a skin problem? What if they needed medicine for their eyes?

His "patient" at the moment was Adolfo. Adolfo told "Dr. Tarak" that his shoulder hurt. He wanted pain pills. But Tarak wanted him to see a doctor face-to-face. Perhaps he needed X-rays. He told his "patient" that taking pain pills might not help his shoulder. Tarak then found a list of doctors in Garnet who specialized in the kind of pain Adolfo was having. He gave his "patient" a doctor's name and a telephone number to call.

After everyone had "seen" at least three "patients," the new telemedicine doctors were done for the day. Tarak was very tired. Not being able to sleep was catching up with him. Perhaps he would sleep better tonight.

He and Rick got into Rick's car to look at the pay telephone on Thirty-Fourth Street. On the way, Rick asked Tarak if he wanted to buy a car.

"Something small," Tarak said. "That's what I'm used to driving in India. But driving on the right side of the road like an American? Oh dear, dear, dear. In India we drive on the *left* side. Sort of." Rick laughed at that.

Then Rick said, "Is this where you said the pay telephone was?" He pointed at the dry cleaner and laundry service. He pulled over so they could get out and look.

Tarak and Rick got out of the car and walked to where the pay telephone should be.

Rick looked at Tarak. He said, "I see the booth, but I don't see a telephone. Is this what you were talking about?"

Tarak looked. It was just an empty old phone booth! The windows were broken and dirty. The light was broken. The booth hadn't been used in years. Where the pay telephone should be was just an empty space. Tarak felt his jaw drop. What had happened?

CHAPTER SIX

Tarak was so shocked he couldn't speak. Finally, he said, "There's been some kind of mistake."

"No man, it's fine. It would be easy to see the booth and think there was a pay telephone inside," Rick said. "It's interesting that there's a phone booth here at all. I thought they would all be gone by now. Maybe the phone company just forgot this one." They both went over to look closer.

"Yeah," Rick said. "This dry cleaning business looks like an old gas station." He looked at the long roof that hung almost to the edge of Thirty-Fourth Street. "Look how big the area is, under that roof. The gas pumps would go right there, I think." He turned back to the old phone booth. He pointed at some pipes sticking out of the ground. You could hardly see them. They were covered by dead grass and dirt and trash. He said, "This is probably where people checked the air in their tires. This pipe was for air if they wanted to fill their tires up." He pointed to a second pipe. "Over here might have been water. To put in their engines. That's what they used thirty, forty years ago. It makes sense they would have a pay phone here. You stop for gas, air, water, whatever. You call a friend to tell them you're on your way over."

Rick looked at Tarak. Tarak was still standing and staring at the dead, forgotten phone booth. His face was completely red. "Are you OK?" Rick asked.

"Not really," Tarak said. "It's just that I saw something very different last night."

Rick said "Oh?" He waited for Tarak to say more.

Tarak decided to say nothing about what he had seen. The bright white light of the phone booth. The black, new-looking pay telephone inside. The two people he had seen using it. They put in coins. They dialed a number. They talked to someone. Tarak was sure of it. But if he told Rick these things, Rick might say, "You're just stressed by being in a new country. You're probably not getting enough sleep!" Even worse, Rick might *think* Tarak was crazy. The thing was, maybe Rick was right. Not that Tarak was crazy! But he *was* stressed out, with everything in America being so new. And he was not sleeping well. He wondered if he would sleep at all tonight. He felt really mixed up. Could he be *that* wrong about what he had seen last night?

Rick told Tarak he had to get home to his wife. "Let me drop you off at your apartment," he said. They made plans to go to a used car dealer on Friday. Tarak could start looking for a car. Tarak was so tired. He really needed a good night's sleep.

Of course, that was not what happened. Around 10:00 p.m., the late Texas sunset faded in the west. When it was cool enough, Tarak went out to his balcony to watch the night come. He had a chair to sit on. He was so comfortable. He felt sleepy at last. He let his head hang back. He stretched his legs out. And then suddenly he was wide awake. What? What happened? He sat up. It was full dark. How long was he asleep?

He felt his way into his dark apartment. He found a light and turned it on. The clock showed 2:00 a.m. Of course. His mind still thought it was lunchtime in Mumbai. He could almost taste a nice spicy curry lunch! His busy, busy brain was still not on Texas time. Tarak sighed. It was just one of those things. He turned the light off again and stood for a few minutes in the dark.

Tarak wasn't sleepy at all, now. He ought to walk to Thirty-Fourth Street again! He wanted to find out about the pay telephone. How could the phone be new, and used by real people one night, and then the next day not be there at all? He felt foolish and confused. But he had nothing to lose. It was just a short walk away. Tarak left his apartment and took the same dark road lined with small houses. He passed the same one or two houses with their lights on. As he walked in the cool darkness he had another thought. During his short sleep, he had been dreaming about Diya. That was odd. Thinking about his ex-wife was something he did not like to do. Diya was the reason he was here, in America.

CHAPTER SEVEN

While Tarak walked to Thirty-Fourth Street a wind came up. Last night it had been completely quiet. Tonight was different. The wind made the trees move. As Tarak got to the corner of Thirty-Fourth Street he could see puffs of dust blowing down the empty street. An empty plastic bottle rattled along, in front of the wind. He looked to his left to see the long line of traffic signals far down Thirty-Fourth Street. The traffic signal closest to him was working tonight. Perhaps during the day a crew came to repair it. The traffic light was green. Then it turned yellow, then red, and then back to green. The traffic light moved in the night wind.

The wind blew a puff of dust at Tarak. It made his eyes water. When he got his eyes clear he walked to the traffic light. He wanted to cross Thirty-Fourth Street to see the spot where the phone booth was. Of course it would be just an empty phone booth with broken glass. It would be filled with dirt. Of course it would be just darkness, next to the dry cleaner and laundry service. Of course. But as soon as he got close enough, Tarak saw several things. As he looked from one thing to another, he felt his stomach sink.

First, the traffic light cut out. Just like last night. It was as if someone turned off an electrical switch! *Whump!* Suddenly, this little corner on

Thirty-Fourth Street got dark. Second, Tarak saw a car parked across the street. It was in front of the dry cleaner and laundry service. It was a sports car, low and fast looking. Its top was down. The driver could enjoy the cool night air. And where was the driver? That was the third thing. The driver, an old man, was *using* the pay telephone. And fourth, the phone booth was brightly lit. The phone booth glass looked new. There was no trash, no dirt, no dead grass.

How could that be? Tarak thought. He felt a little cold inside. Truth to tell, he was excited, too. But this couldn't be right. He must have the wrong place. This was not the same phone booth he saw during the day with Rick. He looked at the dry cleaner and laundry service again. It was the same business! He was in the right place!

Tarak crossed the street. He wanted to look at the phone booth more closely. The old man was talking to someone, that was for sure. Tarak could hear him. The old man turned a little and saw Tarak standing there. He didn't seem surprised. In fact, he gave Tarak a little wave and a smile. It was like he was saying, "Just a few minutes more, OK?" It was something Tarak had once seen in an old movie. Before cell phones, when people used pay telephones and had to share them.

Within a few minutes, the old man came out of the phone booth. He was wearing expensive dark slacks and a light shirt with buttons. Tarak could see a big gold watch on his wrist.

"Sorry to keep you waiting," he said. He got into his sports car and started it.

Tarak called over to him. He asked, "What is this place?"

The old man called back, "It's the night telephone. Is there someone you want to call?" He waved and pulled away. He drove off into the night.

Tarak watched as the car went down Thirty-Fourth Street. He was almost afraid to, but he turned slowly to the phone booth. It was bright, with a friendly, clear light. He stood looking at the black, new-looking pay telephone inside. It had an old-style rotary dial. There was a place to put in coins. In fact, someone had left a few coins on the small shelf inside the phone booth. It was a small present left by some caller. Perhaps the woman with the dark glasses? Or the skinny tall kid from last night? Or the old man just now? Tarak didn't know. He just stood there, completely confused. And as he wondered what to do, the phone began to ring.

CHAPTER EIGHT

Tarak could not believe what was happening. He was in Garnet, Texas, a place no one in India had ever heard of. He was alone, in the middle of the night. The street he stood on was dark and empty. He was next to a phone booth that should not be there. Inside this phone booth was an old-style black pay telephone. It was the kind of telephone no one ever saw anymore. And the pay telephone was *ringing*. Tarak looked around. Was the telephone ringing for someone else? He didn't think so. Thirty-Fourth Street was still empty. Cool puffs of wind pushed past Tarak's face.

The telephone kept ringing. Finally,

Tarak walked over and went into the phone booth. The phone booth door folded back like a fan. The floor was clean. There was no dirt and no trash. It looked almost new. He reached over and picked up the black telephone receiver. The receiver was heavy. He put it to his ear. At first he heard a sound like a radio between stations. He pulled the receiver away from his ear a little. Then he heard a woman's voice. The woman said, "Who's this? Who's there?"

Tarak said, "Hello? I am here. Who is this?"

The woman didn't give her name. Instead, she asked, "Tarak? Tarak! Is that you?" The woman's voice became high and sharp.

Tarak opened his mouth but no

words came out. He knew that voice. He knew that high, angry sound. It was from a woman who never had time to talk. A woman who was always angry about something. My god, was that *Diya*? Was that his ex-wife? How could *she* be on a pay telephone in the middle of nowhere? Tarak almost dropped the receiver. The woman continued to speak. She said, "Tarak, I don't understand. Why did you call me?"

This was crazy. Tarak must be dreaming. But he said, "Is this *Diya*?"

There was dead silence on the phone. Then the woman said, "Of course it's Diya. You called me yesterday. I saw it on my cell phone. I'm going to start telling my friends! This is so unfair, to keep calling me."

Finally, Tarak was able to speak. He said, "Wait! I did not call you."

"You did! My telephone says 'two missed calls' from an American telephone number. It had to be you," Diya said.

"No, no," Tarak said. "I did not call you. I do not have a telephone yet."

"Well, you're messing with me," Diya said. "I don't like it. I'm in the office! I'm at work! My cell phone rang and no one answered. Then you came on the line. Why are you doing this?"

Tarak was getting angry. "Diya, listen. I did not call you. It is the middle of the night here. I do not have a telephone."

"Then how are you calling me now?!" Diya asked.

"This is a pay telephone," Tarak said. "I was here and it started ringing."

"Do you expect me to believe that?" Diya shouted. "Oh!" she breathed out. Then she said, "That's enough! I'm hanging up. Do you want me to tell everyone what you're doing? Because I will! I'll tell your family and all my friends!"

"I did no—," Tarak said. But Diya had hung up. Tarak was now listening to an empty line. Tarak hung up the receiver and left the phone booth. He checked his watch. It was 2:30 a.m. He was shaking. It was strange enough to be answering a pay telephone in the middle of the night. It was even stranger to find his ex-wife on the other end of the line. How could that be! And why now? He never thought about Diya. At least, he tried not to. It was not a good marriage. And the divorce was a really, really bad one. By the end of it, all Tarak had left was his job at the hospital. He had to move in with his beloved cousin Chani and her husband Maku.

Tarak took a deep breath. He needed to get back to his apartment. He needed to think about what had happened. He had no answers for any of it.

He walked back home through the darkness. The wind had stopped. It was calm and cool. Tarak thought he would not sleep, not after the conversation with Diya. But in fact, he slept very well, at least for a few hours.

CHAPTER NINE

Tarak was a few minutes late to the morning session at Doctor's Choice Telemedicine. This morning he walked to Thirty-Fourth Street from his apartment. He had seen a coffee shop the day before, when he showed Rick the phone booth. He walked there this morning. Tarak almost never drank coffee. But this morning, he wanted some. He wasn't so tired. That surprised him, after talking with his ex-wife on a mysterious pay telephone at two in the morning. Today, he felt like looking around his new town, during *the day*. Going for coffee was one way to do that.

The coffee shop was small. Through the big glass windows, he could see two workers and a few customers. He put on his mask and went inside. He bought two coffees to go, one for him and one for Rick. He talked for a few minutes with a young man sitting at a table. The young man was studying to pass a test to become an elementary school teacher. He learned Tarak was going to a training session at an office fifteen minutes away. He offered to call a taxi for Tarak. "I'd take you myself, but I'm on my bicycle today," he said. He also pointed out a nearby cell phone dealer on Thirty-Fourth Street. He had bought a cell phone there just a few months ago. "They're good guys," the young man said.

Tarak's taxi arrived. The driver saw Tarak's mask when he got into the back of the taxi. She reached over and put her own mask on. On their way to Doctor's Choice Telemedicine, they passed the dry cleaner and laundry service. Tarak saw it out of the corner of his eye. He chose not to look up. He did not want to see the place in the daytime. Would he see an empty phone booth with broken glass and dirt and trash heaped inside? Or would he see the night telephone, black, new, clean, and ready to use? He did not want to know. Not just yet. He could not explain anything he had seen.

He got to Doctor's Choice Telemedicine and went into the main room. He saw Rick and handed him his coffee.

Rick opened his eyes wide. He said, "Oh wow, thanks man. Just what I needed." He wiped off the cup with a small cleaning wipe. He slipped off his mask and took a sip of coffee.

CHAPTER TEN

The morning was spent in test preparation. The big test would be that afternoon. The new doctors had to show they could use the technology. They had to show they could communicate with patients over the computer. It was very strange to give medical care this way. Tarak wasn't sure he liked it. Working in the Royal Mumbai Hospital was hands-on. You saw a hundred patients each day. But you were face-to-face with them. You could tell a lot by seeing a patient's eyes. Or by looking at how a patient stood or walked. Tarak also missed the big staff of the hospital. There were other doctors, and nurses, lab workers, cooks, and cleaners. Tarak knew quite a few of them.

He wondered what it would be like giving medical care to patients from his own apartment over a computer. He would be at home all the time. He wouldn't see anyone to just talk, or make a joke. He thought to himself, "Well, I will do this for a year. When the virus has passed, I can work in a doctor's office in Garnet. Or maybe at a hospital in another city." With a small shock, he saw that his thoughts and plans were not about India. They were about *America*.

They did practice tests all morning. Tarak felt good. When it came time for his big test in the afternoon, he did well. He saw a real patient. It was

a lady in Oklahoma. She was cough-
ing. She looked very tired on the computer screen. Tarak was worried about
her. Could she have the virus? Or could
it be something else? Maybe just a cold?
Tarak didn't think so. He asked the lady
if she had a fever. She said she did. He
wanted to know if she was having trou-
ble breathing. She said "No, but I'm
so tired. I just want to lie down all the
time. Do you think I have the virus?"

Tarak answered in a slow, clear
voice, "Without a test, we can't know.
But I am worried about this cough you
have, and the fever. I think you ought
to telephone your regular doctor. Let
her know you are sick and that you
want to come in for a test. You should
wear a mask when you go in. And I

want you to go *today.* This is important. You should call them right away. Please don't wait."

"OK, I will," the lady said. She coughed. The computer connection went off.

The Doctor's Choice Telemedicine trainer was an older doctor. She came into the room and said, "That was good communication. I read your file. You were working at a large hospital in Mumbai. Right now, telemedicine might seem silly to you. You can't really see the patients. Maybe that doesn't feel right to you. But I think you just helped that patient. Don't forget that."

CHAPTER ELEVEN

Everyone at Doctor's Choice Telemedicine was feeling pretty good. The big test was over. Everyone passed! In a few days Lori would return to Chicago, and Mark to Boston. Neither of them wanted to fly home. The virus was scaring them. They didn't want to be inside an airplane with a lot of people. They were talking about renting a big car. They would drive together to Chicago. Then Mark would drive on alone to Boston. He had a college friend in Pittsburgh. He would stop there for a night or two. He had never visited Pittsburgh and wanted to see it.

"My friend has an empty apartment I can stay in," Mark said. "That way we can't pass the virus on to each other. We'll get dinner together outside somewhere. Then I can crash at his apartment for as long as I want!"

Tarak talked to Adolfo for a few minutes. Adolfo was a native speaker of Portuguese. He had not begun learning English until he was thirteen. Adolfo had a tough time with the practice test. He spoke very fast. Some of his words were not clear. The "patient" had a hard time catching his questions. The head trainer talked to Adolfo and they did some extra practice. The trainer got Adolfo to slow down. Adolfo also made a list of words the trainer told him sounded unclear. Adolfo's communication was not perfect. But he improved enough to pass the test.

"Do you know where you want to

live?" Tarak asked Adolfo. Adolfo, like Tarak, had left his home country. Tarak wondered how Adolfo felt about staying in the US.

"I have an aunt and uncle in Dallas," Adolfo said. "I'll go there for a few weeks. They want me to move there, get an apartment. But I don't know. San Antonio sounds pretty interesting! More history, more culture, and maybe better jobs!"

Tarak and Rick planned to spend the rest of the afternoon looking for a car. Rick knew a used car dealer on the east side of town. It was called El Caminito. This meant "The Little Road" in Spanish. They found it. They had about forty cars for sale, some old and some new. Tarak liked a small silver car with two doors. It had forty thousand miles on it but it was only two years old. It was perfect on the outside. The inside smelled fresh. The seats were soft and blue. As soon as Tarak stopped to look at the car, a salesman came up and asked if he could help.

Tarak asked, "How did you get here so fast?"

The young man answered, "Oh, it's my job. I can move pretty fast if I have to. Now, what can I tell you about this sweet car? It's in perfect shape. It had only one owner."

In less than five minutes, Tarak was in the car. He gave it a test drive. Rick was in the passenger seat. The car was small, but fast. A few times, Rick checked his seat belt.

"Are you quite all right?" Tarak asked.

"Uh, yeah," Rick said. "It just worries me that you might still try to drive on the *left* side of the road!" Tarak laughed. Rick did not.

Tarak wanted the car. When he got back to the car dealer, he asked to see the owner. They could talk about price. The young car salesman took Tarak and Rick to the car dealer office. As they walked inside, Tarak noticed a large, dark, quite beautiful car parked on the side. Did he know that car? He felt like he had seen it before.

"Here's the owner," the young salesman said. A dark haired lady stood up behind her desk. She put on a blue mask. Even with the mask, Tarak could see her smile. Tarak could not believe it. He was pretty sure he knew her! It was the lady he saw during his first night walk! She knew about the Thirty-Fourth Street night telephone!

CHAPTER TWELVE

The owner of El Caminito was a nice-looking lady in her early thirties. Her dark hair hung down her back. She was ready to do business. She was ready to sell Tarak a car. They both sat down. Tarak saw a pair of dark glasses on the lady's desk. It was really her! She had been at the night telephone on Thirty-Fourth Street! Tarak had so many questions. How did she know about the night telephone? Who was she talking to? How did the night telephone work?

"Are you all right?" the lady asked. "My salesman tells me you're interested in the little silver two door? It's a fine car. I can give you a fair price on it."

"Ah, y-yes," Tarak said. "Sorry about that. It's just that I think I've seen you before."

"Oh?" The lady said. "I wonder where? Well! How interesting!" She looked at Tarak for a minute. Then she said, "Anyway . . . my name is Larissa Montez. And you are . . . ?"

Tarak told her his name. He told her about his new job in Garnet. He told her the name of his apartment complex.

"I know that complex," Ms. Montez said. "It's brand new. How do you like it?"

"So far, so good," Tarak said. "It's quite close to Thirty-Fourth Street. I walk there sometimes."

Ms. Montez smiled and said, "It's an interesting street. One of my favorites.

It is truly original to Garnet. Now . . . let's talk price on this silver two door."

Within twenty minutes, Tarak was the new owner of a silver two-door car with blue seats. Later, Tarak laughed about how he bought the car. Ms. Larissa Montez was a born car saleswoman. She was friendly and nice to talk to. And she got cars sold.

Rick told Tarak he needed to get home. Would Tarak be all right if he left? Tarak told him he could drive himself home, in his new car.

"See you later then," Rick said.

Tarak followed him out of the car dealer office. He said to Rick, "You know, you've helped me so much. I can't thank you enough. Can I do something for you?"

"Get a cell phone!" Rick laughed. "Then we'll talk about it!" He drove off.

The car salesman was doing paperwork for Tarak's new car. Tarak asked the young man, "Could I talk to Ms. Montez again? Is she still here?"

The young salesman pointed to Ms. Montez's office. "She is indeed," he said.

Tarak went to Ms. Montez's office and called through her door. "Might I talk to you a little?" Tarak said.

Larissa Montez looked up from the work on her desk. She slipped her blue mask back on. "Sure, what's up?" she asked.

Tarak sat down. He said, "I remember where I saw you."

Ms. Montez just looked at him. A few seconds went by. Then she nodded.

She said, "Let me guess. You saw me the other night on Thirty-Fourth Street."

Tarak sat back in the chair. He was having surprise after surprise today. Finally, he just nodded his head. "I couldn't sleep," he said. "I have terrible jet lag. My brain still thinks I'm in India. So a few nights ago I was up at 2:00 a.m. I didn't know anywhere else to go. So I walked to Thirty-Fourth Street."

"Uh-huh," Ms. Montez said. "Tell me what you think you saw."

"Well, I'm pretty sure I saw you drive up in that big car that's outside," Tarak said. "I saw you get out of the car. You were wearing dark glasses. Just like those on your desk. You went to an old-style phone booth. It sounded to me like you were talking with someone on the telephone."

"Yes. That was me. The place near the dry cleaner?" Ms. Montez said.

"Yes," Tarak said. "May I ask . . ." Tarak stopped. It was a rude question. He was not sure how to ask.

". . . Who I was talking to?" Ms. Montez finished.

"Yes." Tarak said.

"I talked to my mother," Ms. Montez said.

CHAPTER THIRTEEN

For Tarak, the conversation with Larissa Montez was a strange end to a very strange day. It all started with a really bad conversation with his ex-wife. At 2:00 a.m. just this morning, he was standing on a dark street in a strange town in a foreign country. He was looking at a black pay telephone that should not be there, and the telephone rang. He answered it. And it was Diya. Of all the people on earth who could call, it was his ex-wife back in India. It was a conversation he did not start, and one that he did not want to have. But somehow, through the night telephone, he got connected to her. Just this afternoon, he took a huge test at Doctor's Choice Telemedicine. He passed! He could start his new job in America on Monday morning. And then, only a few hours later, he was the owner of a fast silver two-door car.

Now, here it was, almost 7:00 p.m. He was talking to a very pretty car dealer. Ms. Montez knew about the pay telephone on Thirty-Fourth Street! She had even used it.

Tarak asked, "Do you have a special name for it?"

Ms. Montez answered, "Well, no. I suppose I could call it a night telephone. I've only been there at night." She sighed. Then she said, "I'm not sure how much more I want to say. It sounds so strange talking about it to another person."

Tarak said, "I have seen it twice at night. I have seen three people using it. And two of them spoke to me. One of them called it a night telephone, too."

Ms. Montez said, "Huh! Really!"

Tarak said, "Yes! And that is not all. I was there at 2:00 a.m. this morning."

"Uh-huh," Ms. Montez said.

Tarak said, "Yes, there was an older man. He finished his call and we spoke. Then he left. As soon as he was gone, the pay telephone started to ring."

Ms. Montez sat forward quickly. "*What?*" she said, a bit sharply.

Tarak said, "Yes. I thought it was really, really strange. But there was no one there to answer it. I let it ring for the longest time, and then I answered.

It seemed the easiest thing to do. A phone rings, you answer. Right?"

Ms. Montez was looking at him closely. She held her hand up against the side of her head. Tarak had to think about what to say next. He didn't know Larissa Montez. He didn't know what she would think if he told her it was his ex-wife on the pay telephone.

It was one thing to answer a ringing pay telephone and have a stranger on the other end of the line say "Hello?" That wasn't so crazy. It could happen. It was *another* thing completely if the person on the other end of the line was your ex-wife! Who lived in another country. Who hadn't spoken to you in over a year. Who had no idea you were in Garnet, Texas! It didn't seem possible.

Finally, Tarak decided just to tell Ms. Montez everything. He told her about hearing a sound on the telephone line, like a radio between stations. He told her about his shock at hearing his ex-wife's voice. "I haven't spoken to her in over a year," Tarak said. "It was a very bad breakup. She seemed to think I had called her. But that was not the case. I don't even know her telephone number in India. How could I call her? I just don't understand it. A pay telephone rings in the middle of the night and it's my *ex-wife*?"

Neither Tarak nor Ms. Montez said anything for several minutes. Then Ms. Montez said, "Well, perhaps you should call me Larissa. Especially when you hear what I have to say next. Let's go outside. I don't want anyone else to hear."

They went out the front door of the car dealer office. It was still hot, but the sun was low in the west. They stood near the big, beautiful, dark car that Tarak had seen two nights before when Larissa was using the night telephone.

Larissa saw Tarak looking at the car. She said, "This was my mother's car. She bought it in 1980. I've been keeping it up. Everything in it is original."

"It's a beautiful car," Tarak said. "She must be very happy that you drive it and keep it looking so fine."

"She might be. I hope so," Larissa said. "But I have to tell you. My mother died ten years ago."

CHAPTER FOURTEEN

Tarak didn't think the day could get any stranger. But now it was. Larissa Montez just said that she used the night telephone to talk to her mother. A woman who was dead! Tarak's brain went into a sort of freeze. He did that sometimes. He would stop talking. He would stop whatever he was doing. He would shut his eyes so he could think.

His thoughts now went like this: As a doctor at a big hospital in India, Tarak had known many people who died. He fought hard against their deaths. But sometimes people died anyway. After a few years, he started to focus on the family members who were left behind.

In some ways, they needed just as much help. They could not believe their mother, father, sister, brother, wife, or husband had died. Many times they would sit next to the empty hospital bed for a few hours. If Tarak had time, he would sit with them. They would talk about conversations they had only the day before with the dead person. "Oh she was just telling me about her new cell phone," or "He told me he needed clothes picked up from the laundry service. I suppose I shall go to pick them up now," were some of the things they said.

Tarak remembered one time where a man's youngest daughter had just been accepted into a top college. Her father, who was very sick, was so proud of her. When he died in the hospital, the young daughter said over and over, "He said he was proud of me. He was happy for me. He said so. What shall I do now?" Her mother answered, "You will go to college, just like your father hoped. We will find a way."

CHAPTER FIFTEEN

Larissa Montez watched Tarak Kapoor. He looked a little white in the face. But by the way he stood, he was thinking hard about something. His arms were crossed. His head was down. She didn't think he would fall over or get sick. What she told him was pretty shocking. She decided to say nothing. To give him some time.

In a few minutes, Tarak changed the way he was standing. His head came up. His arms went down to his sides. He looked at Larissa with his clear brown eyes. He took a deep breath.

"I wonder," he said, "what do you talk to your mother about?"

Larissa laughed in surprise. What an interesting question! Then she said, "Sometimes I need a recipe for soup. Or I'm looking for something in the house and I can't find it. I called her once after I broke up with my boyfriend."

"So you are talking to her about everyday things. Small sorts of things," Tarak said.

"Well," Larissa said, "I wouldn't call breaking up with a boyfriend a small sort of thing."

Tarak laughed. His face had more color. He wasn't as white and shocked as he was a few minutes ago.

Larissa continued, "Mostly, when I call, I hear static. Like you said, a sound like a radio before you find a station.

But sometimes I hear a woman's voice. I can't always hear words. But I think it's her."

"What did you call her about the other night?" Tarak asked.

Larissa frowned. "I'm getting scared and tired, what with the virus. It's hurting my business. My aunts and uncles are old. They're hiding at home. They can't go out. They're so sad and lost. Their kids live in Dallas or Houston so they can't help. So I'm taking food over, or taking them to the doctor. And one of my salesmen got sick last week. We had to spend four hours cleaning everything in the office. One of my uncles is coming over tomorrow to clean the insides of all the cars in the lot. I'm trying to find him things to do. I'm trying to find a little money to pay him. He was closest to my mother. She was his big sister."

"How do you make the call?" Tarak asked. "What number do you dial?"

"Oh, just the phone number from when I was a child. 583-0210," Larissa said. "I was out driving one night a few months ago. I couldn't sleep. I saw the phone booth. Its light was on. I'd never seen it before. I must have driven past it hundreds of times. I just never saw it until then! I was missing my mother a lot that night. So, I stopped my car. I went up to the phone, and without thinking about it, I just dialed my old telephone number. And my mother picked up!"

Larissa stopped talking. Then she said, "You must think I'm crazy."

Tarak laughed. "You must be joking," he said. "Don't forget! I'm the one who got a telephone call from my ex-wife who is very much alive! All the way from Mumbai!"

"Yuck, right," Larissa said.

CHAPTER SIXTEEN

Tarak and Larissa went out for dinner. Tarak followed her to a small Mexican restaurant in his new car. The restaurant had tables and chairs outdoors.

Tarak asked Larissa to order for him. "That way I can be surprised," he said. "I have no idea what to order. Just . . ."

"No beef, right?" Larissa said.

"I'm afraid not," Tarak said. "No beef."

The restaurant owner's husband brought their food out on a tray. Larissa said the two plates were smothered burritos.

"They're made with chicken," she said.

"Ah, fine," Tarak said. "But why 'smothered'?"

Larissa laughed. She said, "The burrito is 'smothered' with sauce. See? The cook pours it over the burrito. So the burrito is covered, or smothered." She took her knife and fork and cut a piece from the burrito. "Hmmm! Nice and soft! Without the sauce the chicken will be too dry."

Tarak paid for dinner. "It's just a small thing," he said. Larissa tried to say no, but Tarak just smiled and shook his head.

Larissa asked Tarak, "Well, what will you do now? You know about the night telephone. Do you think you will try using it again?"

"That is a very good question,"

Tarak said. "And to be honest with you, I don't know."

"Well," Larissa said. "I understand that!"

They said goodbye. Tarak got into his car and drove to his apartment. Tarak sort of knew where he was, and how to get where he wanted to go. He made only a few wrong turns. By the time he got home, it was dark. There was just a touch of orange in the western sky. When Tarak got to his apartment, he got ready for bed. Then he turned off his lights and lay down. Perhaps he would sleep all night this time! He felt tired enough. He should be on Garnet time now, not on Mumbai time. And as it turned out, he *was* on Garnet time. For the first time in two weeks, he slept well. He slept through 2:00 a.m., and then 3:00 and 4:00 and 5:00 a.m.

How many people came to the night telephone as Tarak slept for so many hours? Quite a few! There was Mike, who asked his father if he should stay in college. Mike had a summer job at a roofing company. The company owner liked him and wanted him to stay on in September. Should he quit school and take that job? The answer he got was no. He only had another year to go in college, his father told him. Mike couldn't be a roofer for the rest of his life.

Then there was Candy, who wanted her boyfriend back. When she dialed his number, it just rang and rang and rang. No one answered. And Larissa went. She told her mother about dinner with Tarak. She told her about her salesman getting sick. She said how she was afraid for her aunts and uncles, who were so lost and confused. Oddly, Larissa didn't hear her mother's voice. Instead, she heard a song from Mexico she always loved, "Mi Único Camino." She felt lighter hearing it. She sang the song on her way home, driving through the cool night air.

Tarak slept well that night and for weeks to come. He enjoyed his job at Doctor's Choice Telemedicine. He got out of his apartment once a day to get coffee or to go to the store. With his new cell phone, he texted his cousin Chani sometimes. She told him about friends back in Mumbai, and even once, about Diya. Not that Tarak wanted to hear about her. He met Rick and his wife to share dinner outdoors in a park. He met Larissa, and they took walks in the evening. As they walked they saw people wearing masks. Finally, the message had gotten through to the people of Garnet. The virus was very bad. People had to wear masks and wash their hands.

Tarak did his best to look forward and to live his life. He drove around Garnet. He got to know the city. He started looking for a house to buy. He wanted more space. He wanted to learn how to paint a room, any color he liked. He talked to his father and mother in India. They were well, but they were worried about the virus. They were right to be worried! It was bad just about everywhere. In his telemedicine work, Tarak did his best to take care of patients who needed his help. Even through the computer screen, he could see their fear. He listened, and he answered questions. He ordered medicine. He gave advice.

CHAPTER SEVENTEEN

It was now late October. There had been three days of rain and wind. Summer was over. The nights were now cold and clear. The leaves on the trees started to turn colors. Tarak didn't even know the names of such brilliant colors. This was his first autumn away from India. Larissa went shopping with him to find warm slacks, shirts, and a jacket. It would get very cold soon, she told him.

Tarak bought a house! He was moving into it the next day. Everything he owned was packed into a few boxes. He felt restless on his last night in the apartment. He had a hard time falling asleep. Would the new house be ready? Had the cleaners come? Would he forget anything? Was he making a mistake, buying a new house? In a foreign country? In between these thoughts, he fell asleep. When he next opened his eyes, his bedside clock said 2:00 a.m. Somehow, he was not surprised. He didn't even try to fall back asleep.

He got out of bed and threw on his clothes and his new jacket. He already knew where he was going. As he left the apartment, he grabbed a small notebook from the kitchen table. He patted his pants pocket. He wanted to make sure he had some coins. He would need them for the night telephone. Would it be there, waiting for him? He had not visited since that night he got that awful call from Diya.

He wanted the night telephone to be

there. He wanted it to be there because now he had someone he felt a strong need to call. At the same time, he *didn't* want the night telephone to be there. Such a telephone could not be. There at night and then gone during the day? Not possible!

Tarak got to Thirty-Fourth Street after a short walk. Tonight it seemed the whole world was asleep. All the houses and businesses were dark. It was completely quiet. There were no cars. Tarak only heard the lonely song of a single cricket. Somehow, even with the cold weather, it was still alive.

As he got close to the dry cleaner and laundry service, he saw that the night telephone was there. He let out his breath. It did not fit in a normal daylight world. But tonight, there the night telephone sat, dark and new looking, inside the glass phone booth. Its light was golden and friendly.

Tarak walked up to the night telephone. He opened the glass door of the phone booth. He took some coins out of his pocket. He picked up the receiver and put the coins into the telephone. Then he took out the small notebook and found a Mumbai telephone number. He dialed it. He heard the phone ring and then a woman's sweet voice say, "Hello?"

"Chani!" he said. "My favorite cousin! How are you?"

CHAPTER EIGHTEEN

Chani laughed and laughed. She was at home, waiting for her first baby to arrive. It was due in December. "Oh Tolu!" she finally said. "I was just telling Maku I wanted to call you. I've heard something that you *must* know about!"

"Tolu" was Tarak's family nickname. Chani and Tarak had grown up together as children. They were the same age. Chani loved to talk and talk and talk. She knew everything about everyone. Her dark, round eyes missed nothing. Of all of Tarak's family, Chani was the only one he told about the night telephone. She knew about the phone ringing in the night, and how his ex-wife Diya was at the other end of the line. How Diya had said she would tell everyone that Tarak was still calling her, months after the divorce.

"And what *must* I know?" Tarak asked. He was laughing. Chani had such a love of chatter and talk.

"Well, Tolu, something *interesting* has happened to Diya!" Chani said.

"Diya?" Tarak said.

"Yes, Diya! Do you remember her telling everyone you kept calling her? That you were bothering her from America? That you could not forget her? That you still loved her?" Chani said.

"Um . . . yes . . ." Tarak said. He didn't like where this was going.

"Well! It seems she knew someone in America after all! But not you!"
Chani said.

"What do you mean?" Tarak said.

"She had a secret boyfriend nobody
knew about! Some big banking type in
New York. From a rich family in Mumbai!" Chani said.

"Oh . . ." Tarak said.

"He was already tired of her! He
went to America to get away from her,"
Chani said. "That silly Diya was trying to get a rumor started, using *you*.
If she could tell everyone that you were
still interested in her, that big bank guy
might get jealous! He would be interested in her again! Well, he just got
married! But not to her!"

"Oh my god," Tarak said. "Oh Diya . . ."

"You're not sorry for her, I hope?" Chani said. "It was disgusting, what she was saying about you. Her friends were getting sick of her."

"No, not really," Tarak said. "I guess . . . well . . . the divorce was awful. In a small way . . . I thought it might be my fault."

"Never!" Chani said.

Tarak said, "It's true. But at just this moment, after hearing this from you, I feel free. If I ever had any doubts, they are now gone. Diya just was not a good person to be married to. For anyone, perhaps. I'm sad to say it! But now I must go my way. And she must go hers."

They talked for a few more minutes about this and that. It was hard to stay sad when you talked to Chani. Tarak hung up. He spent a few minutes looking at the beautiful, black, shiny night telephone. He touched it. It was real and solid under his fingers. He reached into his pocket and took out some more coins. He left them on the shelf for the next caller. Just a little present for someone who needed it. Then he walked out into the dark night.